PERCY THE PARK KEEPER

A CLASSIC TREASURY

To Edie
With Love from
Eileen ~ Ken

xx

PERCY THE PARK KEEPER

A CLASSIC TREASURY

NICK BUTTERWORTH

TED SMART

This edition produced for The Book People Ltd,
Hall Wood Avenue, Haydock, St Helens WA11 9UL

First published by HarperCollins*Publishers* in 2004
HarperCollins*Publishers*, 77-85 Fulham Palace Road, London W6 8JB

Visit our website at: www.harpercollinschildrensbooks.co.uk

ISBN 0-00-771297-9

Printed and bound in China

Everyone's Friend
PERCY

PERCY, THAT'S ME!

I'm Percy the Park Keeper. Looking after this beautiful park keeps me very busy. And then, on top of that, there always seems to be some little problem to sort out for a fox or a badger or a mole or a mouse. Still, I do like a bit of fun and mischief too.

I live in my cosy little hut by myself, but I'm never lonely. My friends, the animals, see to that. Aha! That sounds like someone at the door now. I'd better see who it is. Excuse me, won't you? If you head for the big oak tree by the lake, you're sure to bump into one or two of my friends on the way. I'll catch up with you and we can have a bit more of a chat...

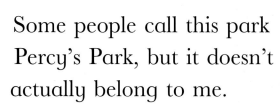

Some people call this park Percy's Park, but it doesn't actually belong to me.

A long, long time ago, when some of the great oaks in the park were just acorns, someone built a magnificent house here. It had lovely gardens, a lake and a wonderful maze.

But one day, there was a fire and the great house burnt down. There are still some bits of it that you can see, but no one would want to live there now.

No, I prefer my old hut. It's quite big enough for me and there always seems to be room for my friends. Sometimes I think it must be bigger on the inside than it is on the outside. Perhaps it is!

I REALLY LIKE . . .

Spring time. I like the autumn too.
But especially the spring. And the autumn.

Stories. I like to read them, but I
enjoy listening to stories on the radio too.
And I enjoy telling them!

I DON'T LIKE . . .

Windy weather. It's exciting for clouds but trees don't like it, and nor does my washing!

Being ill. But once in a while, I have to let others take charge and I just have to take my medicine.

I live on my own, so it's a mystery to me how I get through so much food.

I used to carry a heavy basketful of shopping back from the village shop every week. But one day, the handle of my basket broke and my shopping spilled all over the floor.

Mrs Purvis, the shopkeeper, came to my rescue (the owl thinks she likes me). She helped me to pick up my shopping. Then, she very generously gave me this old delivery bicycle. It makes shopping much easier. When I'm not using the bicycle for shopping, I can take all my friends for a spin around the park. Well, my animal friends, anyway. Perhaps not Mrs Purvis.

I've got lots of pictures in my photo album.

I tried to take a picture of myself with my camera on its automatic setting. I didn't see the molehill

A letter to Auntie Joyce. Hold tight badger! Don't post the mouse!

Here are just a few of me and some of my friends.

This is an old
picture of my
Great Uncle Jack
holding me.
Great Uncle Jack
was a fisherman.
I was a baby.

Guess
Who!

If I'm not in my hut or out in the park, you'll probably find me in my workshop, fixing and mending. I like to invent things too.

Some of my inventions work! Some don't.

My unsinkable boat sank. Luckily, the
mole is a good swimmer. My six-wheeled
barrow was quite good until I bumped over
a log. My five-wheeled barrow was not so
good. I usually get a lot of help when I'm
inventing but it's strange how some help
can actually make things take longer.

A PARK KEEPER'S DREAM

I'm always very busy,
  With lots to do and make.
I think it would be nice, sometimes,
  To have a little break . . .

Of course, I never work at night,
  Especially when I'm sleeping,
But once I had the strangest dream,
  A dream about park keeping!

First I had to comb the grass,
  And then to paint the hedges.
I chose a lovely shade of pink,
  (With purple round the edges).

I planted bulbs along the paths,
  And candles in the beds,
And they were lovely colours too,
  All blues and greens and reds.

All night I dug and raked and hoed,
  Inside the potting shed.
I worked so hard, when I got up,
  I went straight back to bed!

A FAVOURITE PLACE

Can you keep a secret? If you can, I'll tell you about a very special place in the park.

Follow the path by the stream up from the lake. You'll come to a place in the wood where the stream tumbles over a little waterfall. It's where I go when I want to sit and think.

It's a wonderful place to be when the sun is setting. But my favourite time is early in the morning. Mist floats over the pool and the little waterfall chatters away to itself as it sparkles in the early sunlight.

My friends know about this special place, but they usually don't disturb me. Once or twice, I have known a rabbit or a mouse to creep alongside me. Perhaps they wanted to do some thinking too.

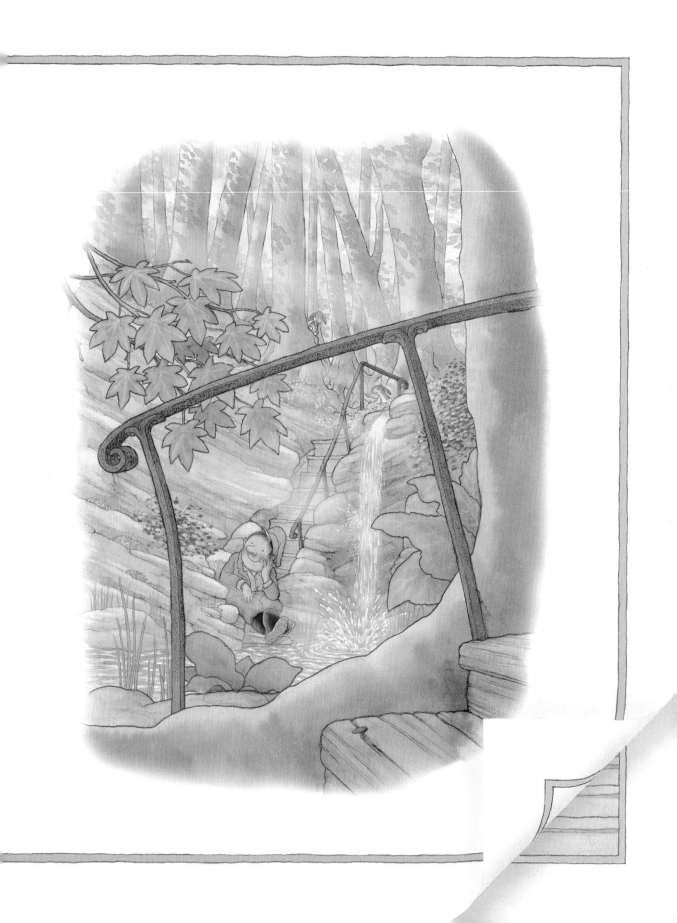

Here is another of my favourite places.
I like to visit my friends' tree house home
every day. I must have left that cheese
roll there yesterday. With the fox living
next door, I'm surprised it's still there!

THE CROSS
RABBIT

It was a bright, cold winter's day.
Snow had fallen in the night and now everything in the park had been turned into a guessing game.

"It looks wonderful," said Percy the park keeper, "but it makes a lot of work."

Standing next to Percy was a rather old and cross looking rabbit.

"Well, quite so," said the rabbit. "But now, what about these mice? They're making a dreadful nuisance of themselves."

Percy found it hard not to laugh
when he saw what was making
the rabbit so cross.

The mice were having great fun.

Percy began to chuckle, but quickly
turned the chuckle into a cough. After
all, this was no fun for an old rabbit
who only wanted to curl up and sleep
through the cold weather.

"Now come along, you mice," said Percy. "You must go and play somewhere else. And," he added, "try to stay out of mischief."

The mice looked very disappointed. Slowly they walked away, dragging their toboggans behind them.

The old rabbit said thank you to Percy and then disappeared into his burrow.

Percy got on with clearing the snow. It was hot work even in the cold weather. First he took off his cap. Then his scarf. And then, even his gloves.

Percy worked hard all morning.
He mopped his brow again and
looked at his work.

"Very good," he said to himself. "I think
I deserve a spot of lunch."

Percy reached for his bag and pulled out a flask.

"That's funny," he said. "I'm sure I put the cup on the top this morning."

"I know, I'll have my yogurt first and drink from the empty carton."

Percy took out a strawberry yogurt and began to rummage through his bag.

"That's odd," he said.

"No spoon. Hmm."

It was a strange lunch. A lid was missing from a small box of dates and the bottom half of one of Percy's cheese rolls had disappeared. And Percy was sure he had packed an orange but there was no sign of it now. It was all very puzzling.

It felt colder to Percy as he went back to work. He reached for his scarf and his cap, but now they had disappeared too!

"This is most peculiar," said Percy. Then, as he gazed around looking for his cap and scarf, Percy was amazed to see his gloves walking off by themselves!

"I must be dreaming," said Percy.

"I'd like to be dreaming," said a cross voice. It was the old rabbit again. "Those mice are making a terrible noise. Would you speak to them please?" And with that the rabbit stumped off.

Percy followed.

"Look!" said the rabbit.

Percy looked. The mice had been very busy indeed! And they were having a marvellous time.

"Hello Percy!" they called. But suddenly they looked worried. "You're not going to tell us to stop, are you?"

Percy glanced at the old rabbit.

"Well. . .no," he said to the mice. "We just wondered if you could have a marvellous time a little more quietly?"

The mice cheered.

"We'll try!" they squeaked loudly.

"Come on," said Percy to the rabbit. "I think I've got some cotton wool in my bag. A little in each ear should do the trick."

ONE WARM FOX

"Shoo! Go on, shoo!" said Percy the park keeper. "This isn't bird seed. Shoo!"

Percy was sowing some wild flower seed on a patch of bare earth. But a bunch of rooks who had suddenly appeared were trying to gobble up the seed as fast as Percy could scatter it.

"And you're not much help," said Percy to a rather saggy-looking scarecrow he had made. He sighed and tried to cover the last of the seed with his rake.

When Percy got back to his hut,
he found his friend the fox sitting
on the steps. Next to the fox there was
a parcel.

"Hello," said Percy. "I see
the postman has been."

Percy picked up the parcel and looked at the writing.

"Oh dear," he said.

"What's the matter?" said the fox. "Don't you like parcels?"

"Not from Auntie Joyce," said Percy. "She knits things. This will be another pullover or a scarf or something. I've got a collection."

Percy began to open the parcel.
"She's very kind," said Percy, "but
somehow, the things she knits...well,
they don't really suit me. Not my sort
of colours. Either that or they don't fit."

"Perhaps they'd fit me," said the fox.
"I was a bit chilly last night."
Percy unwrapped the rest of the parcel.

"Well, this will keep your ears warm,"
he chuckled, and he tossed the fox a
woolly balaclava. "Very nice, but a bit
small for me, I think."

The fox pulled on the balaclava.
He looked a bit disappointed.
"I was thinking more of a pullover,"
he said. "This is squashing my ears."

Percy smiled.
"Follow me," he said.
"Pardon?" said the fox.

"I said follow me," Percy repeated
loudly, and he led the fox into his hut.

Percy brought out an old suitcase from under his bed. He blew the dust off it and opened it.

"How about this?" Percy held up one of Auntie Joyce's pullovers. The fox put it on.

"It fits!" said the fox happily.

"So it does," said Percy with a chuckle.
"In that case, help yourself. I'm just
going to check my wild flower patch."

P ercy wasn't gone for long. As he
walked back towards his hut, he
didn't look too pleased.

But, as soon as Percy opened the door, his face changed.

"Everything fits!" said the fox.
Percy roared with laughter.

"You can't go about like that!" he said.
"Anyway, you'll be much too hot. You'll
cook!"

"It is a bit warm," admitted the fox.
"I just thought, at night, you know..."

"You can keep the pullover," said
Percy, "but I think you should take off
the rest. Besides, I think I know someone
that these things might suit."

The next morning, Percy was out
working in the park when he met
the fox again.

"How were you last night?" asked Percy.

"As warm as toast!" said the fox. "How is your wild flower patch? Are those rooks still being a nuisance?"

"I can't understand it," Percy chuckled.
"They haven't been near the place!"

THE OWL'S
LESSON

Swallows and swifts flew high above the head of Percy the park keeper. Soon they would be off on their long winter holidays. Some birds had already gone.

Percy was thinking how nice it would be to join them, but his thoughts were soon brought back down to earth.

"Percy! Look what we've found!"
    Just ahead of him, a squirrel friend
and the mole were standing over a heap
of twigs.
    "Hello," said Percy. "That looks like an
old nest." He picked it up. "I shouldn't
think anyone lives in it now."

"Then you'd be wrong," said a little voice. A small feathery head stuck itself out from beneath the twigs. "I live in it. And you're holding me upside down."

"I'm so sorry," said Percy. He turned the nest over. "I thought you would have gone with your friends and relations."

"Can't fly," said the little bird. "I didn't get the hang of it."

"Oh dear," Percy began, but he wasn't allowed to finish.

"Good morning!"
It was the owl.

"Owl!" called Percy. "Can you help?
This little fellow can't fly."

"Flying?" said the owl, as she swooped
overhead. "Nothing to it," she hooted,
as she went into an impressive spin.
"Just flap and go!"

The owl shot up into the air and out
of sight. Almost at once, she was back
again, flying just above their heads.

"You see," she cooed,
"it's easy . . ."
"Look out!" shouted Percy . . .

THUMP!
The owl
hit a pine tree.
Pine cones
rained down
on the squirrel
and the mole,

followed by the
owl in a dazed
and untidy
heap.

"Well," said Percy, "I think there's a lesson for us all."

"Percy," said the squirrel, "have you got any string?" Percy felt in his pocket.

"Here's a piece," he said. "Why do you want it?"

The squirrel jumped to his feet. "Come on," he said to the little bird. "I'll give you a piggy-back."

Percy looked puzzled as the squirrel began to climb a tree with a very nervous passenger on his back.

"He needs to get used to heights," explained the squirrel.

W hen he reached the top, the squirrel tied the string between two branches.

"It's a tightrope," he said. "Follow me!"

Balancing carefully, the squirrel stepped onto the string. The little bird bravely followed.

"Hooray!" cheered the mole.

"Well done!" called Percy. "We'll have you taking to the air in no time."

At that very moment, with a twang!
one of the squirrel's knots came
undone and the tightrope walkers
found themselves falling.

The squirrel managed to grab the end of the string. The little bird didn't. As he looked down, he expected to see the ground rushing towards him. Instead, he saw Percy, holding out his cap.

The little bird fell right into Percy's cap, but so hard, that he bounced straight out again.

"Oh no!" shouted Percy. "He's going to fall into those thorn bushes. Fly! Fly!"

And, as if he'd been doing it all his life, that's just what the little bird did. He flew. Away from the thorns, up into the air and perched at the top of the tree.

"Don't stop," called the owl.
"You can go after your friends
and relations now."

The little bird looked delighted.
"I will!" he called back.
"Thank you everybody!"
and with that he was off
over the tree tops.

"Don't mention it," said a voice dangling from a piece of string halfway up a tree. "Don't mention it."

THE LOST
ACORNS

"Mmm! I do love the autumn," said Percy the park keeper. Percy was out looking for a good place to plant the last of his spring bulbs.

"Over there, I think," said Percy. "My daffodils and snowdrops will look wonderful around that holly bush."

As Percy set to work, a robin flew by
and landed next to him.

"Hello, Percy. What a lot of berries!"

"Yes," said Percy. "That means it's going
to be a long, cold winter."

The robin fluffed up his feathers and
flew off with a shiver.

Percy carried on with his work, but then, he stopped and stared at the ground. There was a strange trembling in the earth around the holly bush.

Suddenly, soil burst into the air and one of Percy's bulbs popped out of the ground, balanced on a little pink nose!

"Mole," sighed Percy, "I thought we agreed. No molehills on the grass."

The mole blinked in the sudden daylight.

"Sorry, Percy," he snuffled. "I got lost."

Percy smiled.

"Well, try to dig more carefully in future!"

Percy replanted the bulb.
He still had quite a few
left and so he decided to plant
them around a large oak tree.
But as he knelt down to
start digging, something
hit him on the head.
An acorn!

Percy looked up,
but he couldn't see
anything. Then, another
acorn bounced off his
cap. This time he heard
giggling.

"Come on, then," said Percy. "Show yourself, you rascal!"

A squirrel's head popped out.

"Boo!" she said. "I surprised you didn't I Percy?"

"You certainly did," Percy laughed.

The squirrel scampered down the tree and picked up her acorns.

"What are you doing?" she asked.

"I'm planting my spring bulbs," said Percy.

"Oh," said the squirrel. "I thought you were burying nuts for the winter. I've buried lots and lots."

"It's a good job you have," said Percy. "It's going to be a long, cold winter."

"Well, then," said the squirrel, "I'd better go and bury these last few. I've got an extra special secret hiding place!"

Soon, Percy had finished.

"There!" he said, shaking the soil off his trowel. "Time for tea and buttered toast."

But poor Percy hadn't gone very far when he got a nasty shock. Somebody had been digging up his bulbs.

Percy bent down and picked one up. There were small tooth marks on it. "Someone's been trying to eat my bulbs!" said Percy. "Who would do that?"

Then, Percy heard something, or some*one*. And the someone was not very happy.

Percy peered out from behind a tree.
There was the squirrel. She was digging
up another of his bulbs. She sniffed at it and
took a bite. Then, she threw it away.

"What on earth are you doing?" said Percy.

"Oh, Percy," said the squirrel in a shaky
voice, "I've looked everywhere.
I can't find them . . ."

"There, there," said Percy. "Now tell me, what can't you find?"

"My acorns!" she wailed. "I hid them in a special secret hiding place and now I can't remember where it is!"

"Don't worry," said Percy. "I'll help you collect some more."

"But there aren't any more," she sobbed.

"Well, in that case," said Percy, "we'll just have to go on digging until . . ."

But before he could finish, Percy was interrupted by a strange rumbling noise.

Suddenly, the mole burst out of the ground in a shower of acorns.

"Oh dear," he blinked. "Lost again. Sorry."
But Percy just laughed.

"It looks like the mole has found somebody's extra special secret hiding place," he chuckled.

"Oh thank you, thank you!" said the squirrel. "Now I'd better hide them again. Somewhere really safe."

"Er...not just yet," said Percy. "Not until you've helped replant my bulbs! Then we'll all go back to my hut for tea and buttered toast. Or perhaps you'd prefer acorns?"

THE FOX'S HICCUPS

The first stars were beginning to show in the sky as Percy the park keeper made his way home to his hut in the park.

He had been working hard all day and he was tired and hungry. Now he was looking forward to his supper and a good rest.

As Percy plodded on he saw his friend the fox coming up the path towards him. The fox was on his way home too.

"Good night," said Percy as they
  passed each other.
  "Good night, hic-Percy," answered
the fox.
  The fox had hiccups.

The fox had been drinking some fizzy lemonade when a squirrel told him a funny joke about a parrot, a worm, and a cricket bat.

The fox exploded with laughter. It was then that he had learnt that it is not a good idea to laugh and drink at the same time. He had had hiccups all afternoon.

"I wonder if hic-Percy knows a good cure for hic-cups," the fox said to himself. "I th-hic I'll ask him," he said and with that he turned and followed after Percy.

When he got back to his hut, Percy remembered that he still had one or two jobs to do. First, he watered some plants.

"I'd better get my washing in too," said Percy. "Then, it's two boiled eggs for me and a pile of toast soldiers."

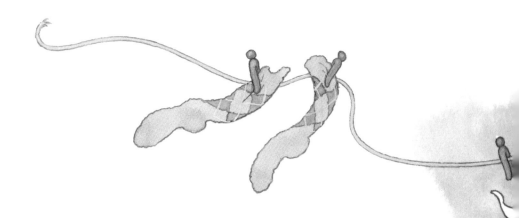

The fox hurried on. He wasn't afraid of the dark. He just liked the light better, that's all. But where was Percy?

He ran round the side of the hut, but instead of finding Percy, he found Percy's washing. Then, with a crash and a tumble which hurt his foot, he found a pile of flower pots.

"Oooowww-hic-ooww!" wailed the fox.

Percy was surprised by the crash. He stuck his head round the corner. But when Percy saw what had made the crash, he quickly pulled it back again.

"It's . . . it's a ghost!" he gasped.

Percy had never met a ghost before. He felt he should introduce himself. But what should he say to a ghost?

Percy listened hard. He could hear the ghost still moaning and thumping about. Suddenly, there was another loud crash, then silence.

Percy was just beginning to wonder if perhaps the ghost had disappeared when there came another sound. A small sound. It was not the sort of sound that Percy expected to hear from a ghost.

"Hic . . . burp."

A smile spread over Percy's face.

Percy poked his head round the corner again. This time, what he saw made him roar with laughter.

"Do you need any help, Mr Ghost?" said Percy, still laughing .

"Yes, please," came a muffled reply from inside the barrel. "Could you possibly turn me the right way up?"

P ercy helped the fox back on to his feet.
"You gave me quite a shock," said
Percy.

"I gave myself one," said the fox.
"But it seems to have cured my hiccups!"

OWL TAKES CHARGE

"Oof, you're heavy," gasped Percy the park keeper. Carefully, he lifted a small tree into his wheelbarrow. "Still, you'll look very nice near my . . . aah, ahh, A-TISHOO!"

"Oh dear," said Percy. "I hope I'm not getting a cold."

Percy began to rake over the bare earth where the little tree had been. Suddenly with a SNAP! his rake broke.

"Oh thump," said Percy. "I'll have to fix you now."

As Percy passed by the playground, he stopped to blow his nose.

"Dear, dear," he sighed. "Look at that. The roundabout needs painting. There's so much to do."

"Hello, Percy," said the owl, suddenly landing next to him. "How are you today?"

Percy sneezed again.

"I think I must have a cold coming," he said.

"Then you should be in bed," said the owl. "Come along."

"Don't fuss," said Percy, "I feel..."

"No arguments," said the owl firmly. "Into bed with you, now."

"But there's so much to do," groaned Percy. "I've got to make a new rake. I've got to plant that tree, and I've got to paint the roundabout..."

"Now don't you worry, Percy," said the owl. "I'll take care of everything."

Percy closed his eyes.

Outside Percy's hut the owl stopped for a moment.

"Now what did he say? Make. Paint. And plant. Yes, I think that was it."

She looked around and saw the little tree and Percy's rake.

"Ah, yes. Tree. Rake. Roundabout."

The owl was very kind but she was not good at remembering things.

"Um, make a tree. No, that's not it. Paint... or was it plant... hmm. I think I might need some help."

A little later, Percy woke up and looked out of the window.

Whatever were the mice doing with that paint pot? And where were the rabbits going with his little tree?

Just then, the owl came to visit.

"What's going on?" said Percy.

"Nothing for you to worry about, Percy," said the owl. "Would you like me to fan you with my wings? You look hot."

Not far from Percy's hut, the fox and the badger were hard at work.

"That should hold it," said the badger as he finished tying a rope around a big piece of wood.

"Let me try," said the fox.

"Not like that!" laughed the badger. "Here, I'll show you . . ."

Next morning, Percy was already up and dressed when the owl arrived.

"You look much better," she said.

"I'm fine," said Percy. "I'm never ill for long. There's too much to do. Now where shall I start?"

"Come with me, Percy!" said the owl, proudly. "We've been helping."

"Hello, Percy!" said the rabbits. "We planted your rake. Just like you wanted."

Percy stood and stared.

"Er, well, it's very kind of you, but I said *make* a rake not plant it."

"Oh no, Percy," said the owl. "It wasn't a rake you wanted us to make."

"What did you make then?" said Percy.

"Come and see," said the owl.

"I don't believe it!" said Percy. "You've made a roundabout!"

"It took us all night," said the fox.

"It's wonderful," said Percy. "But I said *paint* the roundabout, not make one."

"Oh, no," said the owl. "You didn't say paint a roundabout. You said . . ."

Percy looked worried.

"Don't tell me," he said. "You *planted* the rake. You *made* a roundabout. I suppose you must have *painted* my poor little tree!"

"Just like you said!" replied the owl.

At that moment, three giggling mice appeared, carrying a beautiful painting of Percy's little tree.

"Oh, I see!" chuckled Percy. "That's how you painted it! It's lovely. What kind friends you all are."

"Can we go on the roundabout now?" said one of the mice.

"Of course," said Percy. "Let's give it a spin!"

THE HEDGEHOG'S BALLOON

P ercy the park keeper looked up
from his work and gazed in wonder.
"Two red ones . . . a blue one . . . there's a
yellow one . . . and another blue one . . ."

Percy was counting balloons.
"I wonder where they're
coming from," he said to himself.
"Somebody must have had a party."
He put down his trowel and wiped
his hands.
"Well, if nobody wants them," he said,
"I think I'll help myself."

Percy chased after
the balloons as
they floated past him
on the breeze.
It didn't take him
long to collect
as many as he
could carry.
He began
to walk back
towards his
hut, whistling
happily.

Suddenly, Percy stopped. He could hear a faint sound coming from a tree stump nearby. It was not a happy sound.

"Someone's crying," said Percy. "Oh dear." He let go of his balloons and hurried over to the stump.

Sitting on the tree stump, and looking very upset, was a hedgehog. Two mice were doing their best to comfort him.

"Goodness me," said Percy. "Whatever is the matter?"

"It's all these balloons," said the hedgehog.

Then, in between sniffs and sobs, he explained to Percy how he had always loved balloons. The trouble was that he could never have them because they would always burst on his spines.

"It's just not fair!" And the hedgehog burst into tears again.

"You poor thing," said Percy.
He tried to put his arm around
the hedgehog but took it away at once.
"Ouch," he said.
Then Percy took one of his thick
gardening gloves out of his pocket and
put it on. The hedgehog nestled into
his hand.

"I think everyone should be able to play with balloons," said Percy. "And that includes hedgehogs."

He put on the other glove and gently carried the hedgehog towards an old store shed. The two mice followed.

The mice watched Percy through the window. He set the hedgehog down on a workbench and then he took a tin from a shelf. He opened the lid.

"What's Percy doing?" said one of the mice. "What's in that box?"

"I don't know," said the other mouse. "I can't see properly."

The mice didn't have to wait long to find out. Percy picked up the hedgehog and brought him outside.

"There!" said Percy. "A good idea, even if I say so myself! I think those balloons will be safe now."

The mice clapped and the hedgehog beamed. He thought how smart he must look, wearing his corks.

P ercy caught hold of a bright yellow
balloon.

"Here you are," said Percy as he
handed it to the hedgehog. "Your very
first balloon."

The hedgehog took the balloon and
with a great big smile on his face,
he scampered off with the balloon
floating beside him.

"Another satisfied customer," said Percy,
feeling pleased with himself.

Percy turned to go back to his hut. But suddenly, there came a loud BANG!

"Oops!" said Percy. "One of the corks must have come off. It's a good job we've got plenty of balloons!"

"Don't worry," Percy called to the hedgehog, "I'm coming. . ."

THE BADGER'S BATH

The badger had been doing
what badgers do best.
Digging. He'd had a lovely day
and, as usual when he'd had a
lovely day, he was filthy dirty.

"I'm very sorry," said Percy the
park keeper, "but you can't come
to tea like that."

The badger looked disappointed.

"You'll just have to have a bath,"
said Percy.

The badger looked even
more disappointed.

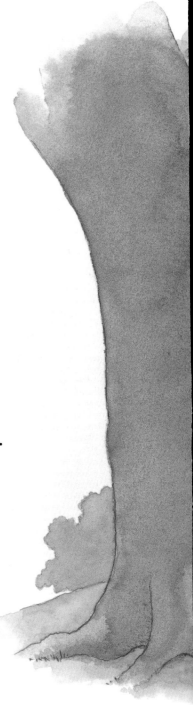

First, Percy filled a tin bath with warm soapy water. Then he brought out all the things that he liked to use himself when he had a bath. Soap, a loofah, his backbrush, a sponge, some shampoo and, of course, his rubber duck.

The badger sniffed at the soapy water. He didn't like it. He didn't like it at all.

Percy thought for a moment. Then he disappeared and came back with a jug which he used for wetting his hair and a shower cap which he used for not wetting it.

"There. I think that's everything," said
Percy. He turned to the badger.
"Now, all we need. . ." But the badger
was nowhere to be seen.

"Hmm. . ." said Percy. "Now all we need
is the badger."

The badger was hiding. He didn't want a bath.

Percy searched and searched but he couldn't find the badger anywhere. He was getting very hot and bothered.

"I really can't understand it," he said. "I always enjoy a bath myself."

Percy sighed as he looked at the bath full of soapy water. Then he had an idea. He went into his hut.

When Percy came out again he was wearing his swimming trunks.

"Well, why not?" he said to himself. He chuckled as he stepped out of his boots and into the bath.

Percy lay back in the warm water and gazed up through the overhanging branches of a tree.

"Silly old badger," thought Percy. "I wonder where he's hiding."

There was a sudden rustling above his head and something black and white moved amongst the leaves. A strange idea came into Percy's mind.

"No. . . surely not?" he said to himself. "Badgers don't climb trees. It must have been a magpie."

The rustling noise came again.

Suddenly, there was a loud CRACK!
With a great howl, a large black and
white animal fell out of the tree, straight
into Percy's bath water. SP-LOOSH!

For a moment, the badger completely disappeared. Then his head popped up through the soap suds, coughing and spluttering.

Percy was spluttering too, but with laughter.

"I see you changed your mind about having a bath," he chuckled. "I suppose you didn't want to miss your tea!"

"I didn't know badgers climbed trees," said Percy.

"Well," said the badger, "we're better at digging." He sighed. "Could you pass me the loofah, please?"

PERCY'S FRIEND
THE OWL

MY FRIEND THE OWL

The owl is really quite clever. But, perhaps not quite as clever as she thinks she is.

She's got brilliant eyesight. But, so often, she still doesn't notice things that are right in front of her beak.

I think her mind wanders. Only the other day I asked her if she thought it was going to rain. Do you know what she answered? You'll never guess. She said, "Twenty-three." You see what I mean?

Still, the owl means well. And she'll do anything to help a friend. Anything at all. As long as she remembers...

Did I say that the owl is quite clever? Well, this was not one of her clever ideas! She thought that if she looked like an eagle, she would be able to fly like an eagle. I'm afraid she was wrong. Unless, of course, some eagles fly into things because they can't see where they're going!

THE OWL REALLY LIKES . . .

To be in charge. But I wouldn't
say she's bossy. I wouldn't dare!

The colour blue. She believes people would
be happier if more things were blue.

THE OWL DOESN'T LIKE . . .

Hats. She says that, generally speaking, they
don't suit her. But she does like party hats.

Foggy weather. She says it is A Danger
To Flying If Conditions Are Foggy.

I wonder if you are any better at noticing things than the owl. This mirror is very strange, it changes things. Can you see nine things that are different in the mirror's reflection? (The owl only spotted four.)

I've got lots of pictures in my photo album.

People with feathers don't usually like sticky things...

The owl tried to show the badger how to tie knots that won't come undone...

Here are some I took of my good friend, the owl.

The owl likes long words. If they don't look right, she just adds a few more letters. And why not?

The owl is very good company - especially if it's getting a bit dark!

The owl once became very
friendly with a cuckoo.
They decided to fly south
together, to somewhere
on the Isle of Wight, I
think it was.

They must have got their arrangements mixed up. She waited on the telephone wires for ages. Eventually, she went to sleep.

In the morning, I found her still holding on. She hadn't noticed that she had swung upside down. We don't talk about it.

THE OWL'S TEA TIMES TABLE

One times two is two.
Two times two is four.
Three times two is...more than that, and
Four times must be more.

Four buns would be two buns each,
If Percy came to tea.
But if the fox came with him,
We'd need another three!

But what if everybody came?
We'd need a lot, lot more.
And tables wouldn't be much use,
We'd all sit on the floor.

FAVOURITE PLACES

I know the owl likes to fly high above the tree tops on a windy day. But when I asked if that was her favourite place to be, she answered, "Not quite."

It seems that
just before take off,
standing on the top
branch of a tall tree
with the wind ruffling
your feathers...well,
the owl says there's no
better place to be.

Perhaps it's a bit like that
lovely moment just before you
take a large bite out of a fresh cheese
and pickle sandwich. Mmm! Yes, I think
I can understand what she means.

The owl lives right at the top of the big
tree house with the other animals. She has
a swing seat up there where she can sit and
watch what everybody else is doing down
below. I wouldn't say she's nosy. Just
very interested in other people.

Here she is, my friend the owl, with what looks suspiciously like my hot water bottle! I wondered what happened to it. It's been missing for a few days. It can't be hot any more, but I expect it's comfy.

PERCY'S FRIEND
THE MOLE

MY FRIEND THE MOLE

The mole spends a lot of his time under the ground but then, all of a sudden, he'll pop up when you least expect him. He usually wears one of two faces. One is smiley. The other looks confused.

We get on well, although we had to have words when he made molehills all over my grass. Now he understands that there are certain places where I don't want him to dig. And I understand that sometimes he loses his way and digs there anyway.

The mole says he has a secret friend called Tootie. He says that Tootie is very clever, but as I have never actually met Tootie, I couldn't say.

The mole doesn't see as
well as the other animals.
It doesn't really matter
because he spends so much
time where it's dark.

He has this funny idea that
dark glasses are for helping to see in the
dark. He found these plastic sunglasses
somewhere in the park. I think he wears
them sometimes when he's digging tunnels.

The fox told him he would be cool in
them. But when the mole wore them
in the sunshine he said they didn't
work. He didn't feel cool.
He felt hot.

THE MOLE REALLY LIKES ...

Swimming! He's surprisingly good at it too.

Spaghetti. As a special treat, I made some
for his birthday. I'm not sure if he thinks it's
food or a game, because he said, "Can we
play spaghetti at my next birthday?"

THE MOLE DOESN'T LIKE ...

Snow. He doesn't mind the cold, but he says it's actually harder to dig through snow than tunnelling underground. I didn't realise that.

Pepper. He has a sensitive nose, poor chap!

The mole is a very kind little chap. When he heard that I had broken my pencil, he decided to get one for me that wouldn't break.

He made it out of an old broom handle.
It doesn't actually write, because the point
is only painted on. But it looks very nice
and it's very, very long. And it certainly
won't break!

I've got lots of pictures in my photo album.

The mole is very good at doing head-over-heels. He can even do it in his tunnels. (Perhaps that's why he so often loses his way!)

The fox thought he had a black snowball – but it was furry – and it had a pink nose!

Here are some I took of my good friend, the mole.

A hot day and a special drink for a special friend.

I was told that Tootie made these muddy footprints. She might be clever, but she doesn't wipe her feet properly.

The Mole isn't afraid of the
dark, but one evening
I heard him talking to
someone who was.

"Yes, Tootie," he said, "it
does look like a monster now.
But what was it before it got dark?"

A little voice, that sounded just a bit like
the mole's, said, "A tree."

Then the mole said, "Well, that's what it
still is. A tree."

Very sensible, I thought.

When I went to say hello
to them, Tootie had gone.

THREE

The mole could never
Possibly,
Count up to more than
One, two, three.
That's why his molehills
Are so many.
He loses count at
Hardly any.
Though forty-nine
There may well be,
The mole will tell you,
"There are three!"

FAVOURITE PLACES

Most of the mole's favourite places are underground and rather dark. He says he likes them because they're cosy and small.

I think I know what he means. On a cold winter's night I like to curl up in my bed with the covers pulled tightly round me.

Actually, I can remember one very cold snowy night when the mole ended up snuggled up in my bed with me. You may have heard about it!

One place I know the mole does like is the
badger's home in the big tree house. They
enjoy talking together about . . . you guessed
it . . . digging!

The mole doesn't live in the tree house. He
has several homes nearby. But now and then
he can be tempted to visit some of the other
animals who live higher up in the tree.
(If you turn over the page you will
see what I mean!)

Here he is, my friend the mole.
I think this squirrel is taking him
to see the view from the top of the
tree. The mole looks like he would
rather have his feet on the ground!

PERCY'S FRIENDS
THE SQUIRRELS

MY FRIENDS
THE SQUIRRELS

Squirrels are bright and quick thinking. They move quickly too and not just over the ground. They seem to be able to whizz straight up a tree as if it were a fallen log!

They like to explore, which can get them into trouble sometimes. I remember an awful kerfuffle once, when a squirrel got stuck in a rabbit hole. Unlike the mole, squirrels are not good at going backwards. I believe it's something to do with bushy tails.

Squirrels can be very forgetful. They never, never seem to remember where they have stored their food. Which reminds me, I put a sandwich down a moment ago. You haven't seen it, have you?

Once, when I was on my way to pick some apples, I noticed three squirrels up in the branches of an oak tree, collecting acorns. I thought how nice it would be, if I could pick my apples like that.

Suddenly, I had a brainwave. My apples could be picked in exactly the same way!

Now, in the autumn, the squirrels help to pick all those apples that are so hard to get at the tops of the trees. And I pick the easy ones that I can reach without having to use my ladder.

It's a very good arrangement. It is strange though. I've noticed a lot more apples have little teeth marks in them than when I used to pick them by myself.

SQUIRRELS REALLY LIKE . . .

Balancing. They seem to be able to balance
on just about anything, although there have
been one or two accidents on my washing line!

Nuts. Not just acorns and beech nuts. They like
peanuts, coconut and hazelnuts too. And they
don't mind if they're covered in chocolate!

SQUIRRELS DON'T LIKE ...

Lightning. I love to watch it myself,
but I suppose it's different if you live at
the top of a tall tree!

Being underground.
Here are two squirrels with their friend,
the mole. Guess which is which!

Everybody loves tobogganing! Well, nearly everybody. Actually, I don't think the owl likes it all that much. And I don't think my Auntie Joyce is too keen. . . But I think just about everyone else loves tobogganing.

The squirrels are especially good at it. Some of their high-speed acrobatics are just amazing.

I think the squirrels would agree though, that their steering of a toboggan is not quite so amazing. In fact, sometimes, it's not at all amazing. It's amusing.

I've got lots of pictures in my photo album.

This palm tree is made from flower pots and fern leaves. The two little monkeys are made from squirrels!

The little monkeys broke my flower pots!

Here are some I took of my good friends, the squirrels.

Squirrels do stop for a rest sometimes. These four were caught napping in my potting shed.

My old wheelbarrow makes a perfect exercise wheel!

The squirrels have great fun playing a game they call 'Acorn Surprise'.
Sometimes it can be called 'Pine Cone Surprise' or 'Conker Surprise'. It just depends what kind of tree they are sitting in.
It goes like this...

They sit quietly on a branch and wait for
somebody to walk underneath. Then they
drop an acorn (or a pine cone or a conker)
onto the person below.

Actually, I had to ask them not to drop
conkers after they dropped some rather big
ones that were still in their spiky cases.
'Conker Surprise' became 'Conker Ouch!'

It's not that far from here to . . .
It's just a short leap through the air.
This tree to . . .
I'll be all right.
I'll grab that branch and hold on tight . . .
The distance doesn't bother me.

I could . . .

The gap that makes me

Hang around

Is the one between me . . .

there

that

somersault it . . . .

see!

and the ground!

FAVOURITE PLACES

The squirrels seem to have quite a few
favourite places. One that I can think of is a
small clearing in the middle of the pine wood
which they call the Mushroom Field. They
call it that because of the lovely big
mushrooms that grow there.

On a misty, autumn morning, if you get
up early enough, that's where you'll find the
squirrels, having a very tasty breakfast!

Now, if I asked what you would expect to find waving in the breeze at the top of a flag pole, the sensible answer would be a flag. You probably wouldn't say squirrels! Not unless you have been to *this* park.

But if you have, you might have seen some of my squirrel friends enjoying the view from another of their favourite places. They tell me there is just enough room for three. Four is a bit of a squash.

I say, there doesn't look to be room even for one! I tell them to be very careful. I suggest that they might be just a little safer leaping through the branches of the big oak tree house which, of course, is where they live.

Here they are, my friends the squirrels.
Are they collecting food here, or are
they just playing a game? Actually, if
I know anthing about squirrels, they're
probably doing both at the same time!

"I was born in London in 1946 and grew up in a sweet shop in Essex. For several years I worked as a graphic designer, but in 1980 I decided to concentrate on writing and illustrating books for children.

My wife, Annette, and I have two grown-up children, Ben and Amanda, and we have put down roots in Suffolk.

I haven't recently counted how many books there are with my name on the cover but Percy the Park Keeper accounts for a good many of them. I'm reliably informed that they have sold more than three million copies. Hooray!

I didn't realise this when I invented Percy, but I can now see that he's very like my mum's dad, my grandpa. I even have a picture of him giving a ride to my brother and me in his old home-made wooden wheelbarrow!"

NICK BUTTERWORTH